The Trouble with Gran

For Rosie, Jim and the boys
(who also come from a tropical planet!)

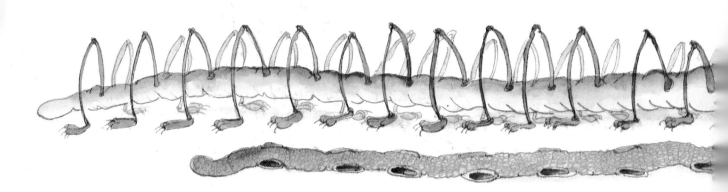

The Trouble with Gran

Babette Cole

Heinemann : London

The trouble with Gran is . . .

None of the other OAP's suspected a thing . . .

. . . until our teacher tried to organise an outing for them, to Wethorp, as our school project!

"But we want to go somewhere hot and exciting!" said Gran.

"Sit down and be quiet!" snapped teacher.

Wethorp was awful.

Gran started to play up!

We went to an Old Time Music Hall.

Gran did not like the singing!

And there was a Glamorous Grandma Contest.

... Gran cheated of course!

She really
livened up
the fun fair!

We were asked to leave the amusement arcade!

On the Lunar Landscape Tour
Gran met some friends.

She took them to
the tea rooms!

So we missed the bus home.

Teacher blamed Gran!

"We've had enough of this dump!" said Gran.
"Fasten safety-belts!"

We zoomed towards Gran's planet . . .

and landed just in time
for carnival!

Gran did the Limbo . . .

. . . and climbed a bloomernut tree.

We were sad to leave,
but Gran had to get home
to feed the cat.

We landed in the school playground with a bump!

Mum and Dad marched Gran away.
"You're too old for that sort of thing now,"
they said.

"That's what they think," muttered Gran.

And when she got home she opened her own travel agency . . .

GRAN TOURS

FLY GRAN

SEE THE WORLD (FROM A DISTANCE!)

. . . in Dad's garage!

William Heinemann Ltd
10 Upper Grosvenor Street
London W1X 9PA
LONDON   MELBOURNE
AUCKLAND   JOHANNESBURG

First published 1987
© Babette Cole 1987
Reprinted 1987

0 434 93296 5

Printed in Great Britain by
W. S. Cowell Ltd., Butter Market, Ipswich